This book
belongs to

_____

_____

For Josh Hughes who really
knows about robots
I.W.

For Martin
A.R.

First published in 2000 in Great Britain by
David & Charles Children's Books
Published in this edition in 2001 by

GULLANE
CHILDREN'S BOOKS

Winchester House, 259-269 Old Marylebone Road,
London NW1 5XJ

5 7 9 10 8 6 4

Text © Ian Whybrow 2000
Illustrations © Adrian Reynolds 2000

The right of Ian Whybrow and Adrian Reynolds to be identified as
the author and illustrator of this work has been asserted by them
in accordance with the Copyright, Designs, and Patents Act, 1988.

A CIP record for this title is available from the British Library.

ISBN 1 86233 210 X hardback
ISBN 1 86233 294 0 paperback

Printed and bound in Hong Kong

Harry
and the Robots

Written by **Ian Whybrow**
Illustrated by **Adrian Reynolds**

GULLANE
CHILDREN'S BOOKS

It was a shock for Harry
when his robot fell over.
It was just doing a nice march
and suddenly its lights went out.

Harry heard Nan coughing in the yard,
so he ran out to show her.

Some of the robot's batteries had leaked onto its wires.
They put him in a parcel and sent him to the robot hospital.
"They'll know how to mend him," Nan said.

Harry wanted to make another robot to play with while he waited for his marching robot to come back.
Nan said, "Good idea. We'll use my best scissors if you like."
They laid the things ready on the table.

But they never got started.
Mum made Nan go to bed,
her cough was so bad.

When Harry woke up the next morning, there was no Nan.
The ambulance had come in the night. She had to go
into hospital, Mum said, for her bad chest.

That day, Sam watched
TV a lot.

Harry started making a robot all by himself.
He wanted to use Nan's best scissors. Nan had said he could.
But Sam said, "No! Those are Nan's!"

That was why Harry threw his Stegosaurus at her.

Mum took him to settle down.
She said he could use Nan's best scissors if
Nan had said so, but only while she was
watching. He had to be very careful
though, because they were sharp.

Harry worked hard
all morning . . .

. . . until there was a new robot. A special one.
    Harry taught it marching. He taught it talking.
    But most of all he taught it blasting.
The robot said,
"Ha - Lo Har - Ree.
Have - you - got - a - cough?
BLAAAST!"

The hospital was big but they found Nan in there.

Mum said Sam and Harry had
to wait outside Nan's room.
They waved through the window
but Nan did not open her eyes.

Sam and Mum whispered with the doctor. So Harry slipped into the room – just him and the special robot.

He put the special robot by Nan.
The robot said,
    "Ha - Lo - Nan.
        Have - you - got - a - cough?"
She opened one eye. It winked.
The robot said,
    "I - will - blast - your - cough.
        BLAAAST!"

That was when Mum ran in saying – "Harry! No!"
But the doctor said not to worry, it was fine.
A robot would be a nice helper for Nan.

That evening, Harry was very busy.

He joined . . .

he stuck . . .

he painted and . . .

Harry made five more special robots to look after Nan.

The robots guarded Nan.
They marched for her.
They blasted her cough.
And soon she was better.

Nan came home and unpacked her things.
"You're a good looker-afterer," she whispered.
"And my special robots," said Harry.
"Oh yes, them too," said Nan.
"I'd like to keep them by me, do you mind?"
Harry did not mind at all.

Nan went out into the yard to see how
the chickens were getting on.
They were just fine.

That afternoon a parcel arrived. It was the marching robot, back from the robot hospital. His light went on and he did a nice march – good as new.